The Rabbit
and the Shadow

Mélanie Rutten

Translated by Sarah Ardizzone

Eerdmans Books for Young Readers

Grand Rapids, Michigan

This is the story of . . .

... a Rabbit
who wants to grow up,

an anxious Stag,

a Soldier at war,

a Cat who keeps having
the same dream,

a Book who wants
to know everything,

and a Shadow.

The Rabbit and the Stag

One day,
the Rabbit appeared.
There was a slight wind.
And a shadow perhaps.

Little ones sometimes appear like that.
Like the wind.

Or sometimes like
a storm.

The Stag had to learn
how to do everything.
But the little one
trusted him.

From that day on,
the Stag watched over him.

When the Rabbit was hurt,
the Stag hurt too.

When the Stag felt anxious,
so did the Rabbit.

When they laughed,
they couldn't tell who started it,

or who had fallen asleep first.

Every morning, they ran a race.
The Rabbit always won.

They walked and gathered sticks
to build little houses with.

One day, the Rabbit would grow up.
    He would go off on his own.

The Stag knew this.
He said, "Run, little Rabbit, run!"
But his heart said, "Not too fast, not too fast!"
Every evening, when they raced back home, the Stag pretended to lose.

Sometimes, at night, the Rabbit was afraid.
"What are you afraid of, little Rabbit?"
"That you won't be here anymore."

So the Stag hugged him.
"Here I am. I love you."
"More than anything in the world?"
"More than anything in the world."
And the world revolved around them.

The Stag told the Rabbit that, in the sky,
the Great Bear danced around her little one
and watched over him.
Always. Even when it was cloudy.

The Soldier

The Soldier was at war.

At war with everything.

He was never at peace.

Suddenly, he heard a hole crying.

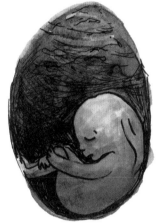

At the bottom of the hole was the Rabbit,
who still had a lot of growing up to do.

"You're crying," said the Soldier. "Are you
on your own?"
"No," said the Rabbit, "and I'm not crying."
"Yes you are! Your eyes are all red! I bet
you need my help."
"No I don't," said the Rabbit.
"Suit yourself then."

But the Soldier came back, and held out his sword.

"It looks like you're mine now," said the Soldier.

"I don't belong to anybody. I want to be on my own," replied the Rabbit.

"Me too! We can both be on our own. But together. It'll be easier that way."

And he dragged the Rabbit off, shouting:
"On our own! On our own!"

The Cat

Farther on,
a Cat was looking
for something.

"Who are you?" shouted the Soldier.
The Cat stood up. He was tall.
"What about you? Who are you?"
asked the Cat. "I bet you don't
even have a mustache!"
But the Soldier didn't want
to take off his helmet.

"The Soldier and I are
forming a team," said the Rabbit.
"A soccer team? I'll join," declared the Cat,
"but I lost my ball in these bushes. Who's going to look for it, I wonder?
I'd say it's a job for a soldier."

In the bushes,
everything was dark.

"Well, what should we do?"
asked the Cat.

"Form a team! We already told you!" replied the Soldier.

"But why?"

"To prove we're not afraid of . . . of . . ." the Soldier began.

"Of climbing volcanoes," said the Rabbit.

"Yes! Of climbing volcanoes!" shouted the Soldier.

The Soldier drew a circle around them.
"What's that?" asked the Rabbit.
"A line," replied the Soldier. "This will be our house."

Night fell.
Nobody saw the Shadow
watching them.

"I made the house, the Rabbit made the fire . . .
what about you, Cat, what can you do?" asked the Soldier.
"Hmm . . . I can tell you a story!" replied the Cat.
"Pff . . . what good are stories?" said the Soldier.
"They help you feel less afraid," said the Rabbit.
"Less afraid of what?" asked the Soldier.
"Of the dark, for example."

The Soldier laughed nervously:
"Ha, who's afraid here?"
"Not me!" said the Cat.

The Rabbit was afraid sometimes.
At night. Not in the daytime.

He had a special way
to feel less afraid,
but he didn't dare say
what it was.

The Book

One day, the Book was attacked by a Soldier,
but he didn't know why.
He didn't like not knowing.
So, to put his mind at ease, he thought
about what he already knew.

He met the Stag,
who was out gathering twigs.
He asked him what he was doing.
The Stag didn't look up:
"They're for my little one.
To build a house with."
"And where is your little one?"
asked the Book.
The Stag replied that he'd gone away.

The Book didn't know what to say.
He wanted to talk about the Soldier,
but the Stag suddenly looked up.
He thought he'd seen
a shadow in the forest.

"I know what this is!" said the Book.
"It's a ball! A basketball!"

The Book was talkative
and interested in everything.
The Stag wasn't really listening.
He was too busy wondering whether
the Rabbit was thinking about him.
And he was remembering
their discussion . . .

The Discussion

"Will we always be together?"
"Yes."
"Forever and ever?"
"Well, one day you'll grow up."

"But we'll still be together!"
"You will always be in my heart."

"Will you die?"
"Not now."
"But one day?"
"One day, yes. It's only natural."

"And will I still be
in your heart, even then?"
"I will always be in yours."

"So we won't always be together," said the Rabbit.

"If we can't always be together, then I'd better learn
how to grow up and be on my own," huffed the Rabbit.
"And another thing, I don't want you to pretend to lose the race anymore!"
"Come on, little Rabbit, let's go home," whispered the Stag.

That evening, they didn't race home.
Up above, the Great Bear was dancing around her little one.
But it was cloudy, and they couldn't be seen.

Alone

It was morning.

"Why don't we leave the Cat behind?" grumbled the Soldier.
"Would you like it if we left *you* behind?" asked the Rabbit.
"No," the soldier answered.
"Well then, we're not leaving the Cat behind."

Something round and white
shone underneath a bush. A ball.
"It's the Cat's soccer ball!"

But it wasn't a ball.
"Look! An Egg!" cried the Rabbit.

"What about my ball?" asked the Cat.
"We need to look after this Egg," said the Rabbit.
"It's none of our business,"
said the Soldier impatiently.
"Leave it. We need to go!"
"No. We're keeping it."

As the Rabbit hugged the Egg,
he felt a stirring in the universe around him.

At a bend in the path,
the whole world opened up.
The volcano rumbled in the distance.

While the Soldier faced great dangers,
the Cat pretended to be a soccer champion,
and the Rabbit looked after the Egg.

Sometimes they hurtled downhill.
At top speed.

Or they waded across
fast-flowing rivers.
Slowly.

Sometimes,
one of them got hurt.

Sometimes
one of them felt anxious.

But when they laughed,
they couldn't tell
who had started it.

Nobody knew
what was in the Soldier's bag
or under his helmet.

At Night

At night, they talked.

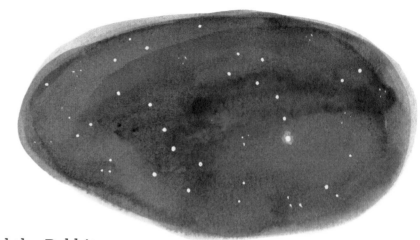

"What's your story, Cat?" asked the Rabbit.
"I have the same dream every night," the Cat replied.
"There's a house full of laughter and light.
The more I run toward the door, the more I shrink.
I can never open it. I'm too small."

"And?" asked the Soldier.
"That's it," said the Cat.
"That's not a story—
it hasn't got an ending!"

Then the Rabbit talked
about building little houses,
like he used to do with the Stag.
And the Soldier talked about his two houses:
his father's house and his mother's house.

"What do you think about
to feel less afraid?"
asked the Rabbit.
"Nice things from the past,"
replied the Soldier,
"like eating rice pudding cake
when I was little."

"You're still little!" said the Cat. "Me, I think
about nice things to come."
"Like when you'll have a mustache?"
teased the Soldier.

The Cat thought about his dream.
They all thought,
for a moment,
about their dreams.

"I've got a special way
to feel less afraid," said the Rabbit.
"I think of the Great Bear
dancing around her little one
without ever leaving.
Up there. In the sky."
"That's babyish!"
mocked the Soldier.

The Rabbit was upset.
"I don't need any of this
to make me feel at home."
He scuffed out the line on the ground.
The Soldier shouted:
"Are you crazy? You . . .
you have to sleep outside then!"

The Rabbit moved away.
Not too far,
not too close.

The Great Bear was there, close to her little one.
The Rabbit wondered whether he was still in the Stag's heart.
He thought about their discussion and dreamed about the volcano.

In the distance, the Shadow was still there.

Growing Up

That morning,
night clung to the trees.
The Cat was dreaming.
A cake, still warm,
was laid out next to them.

The Soldier was asleep
with something in his arms.
As soon as he woke up, he hurried
to hide it in his bag,
but the Rabbit had seen it.

Everybody thought the cake
was strange but delicious.
It was a rice pudding cake.

Today, the volcano
awaited them.

They climbed.
Slowly.
Slowly.

"How can you tell when you've grown up?" asked the Rabbit.
"It's when you can tie and untie knots," said the Soldier.
"No, it's when you're in love," replied the Cat.
The Rabbit thought it was when you knew how to build a house.

"We'll never make it!"
"Never!"
"Never!"

They rested.

The Rabbit leaned over the Soldier and said to him, very quietly:
"I won't say anything. About the secret in your bag."
"Thanks," replied the Soldier.

They set off again.

At last, they reached the top.
"I . . . we did it!" the Soldier
shouted.

"We're champions!"
cried the Cat.

The volcano was spitting fireworks.
"It's beautiful," said the Soldier. He took off his helmet.
"You're . . . you're a girl!" exclaimed the Cat.
"So what if I am?"
"Have you stopped being angry now?" the Cat asked.
The Soldier smiled.

They rushed down the volcano, faster, faster.
"We're not afraid anymore!
Not afraid! Not afraid!"

The Shadow

"We're not afraid anymore! Not afraid! Not afrai—"
This time, they saw it. The Shadow.

"Run for it!" cried the Cat.
The Shadow was moving in a strange way.
"It's going to attack!" shouted the Soldier.
"No," said the Rabbit, "look . . .
she's dancing. She's a mother."

The Shadow *was* dancing.
And without any words, her dance
spoke of the moonlight and the forest.
It spoke of little ones lost and found.
It spoke of how she was the Bear,
the Great Bear of the forest.

The Bear was silent. She could smell the rice pudding cake.
The Rabbit seemed to recognize her.
He decided that she could keep the Egg safe.

The Soldier wanted to go back to her houses,
the Cat was happy where he was, and the Rabbit decided
there was something left to do.

The Bear watched over them.

Together

Later, they noticed a Book juggling
something round and white.
The Cat jumped with joy:
"My ball!"

The Book told them that he'd met a Stag
who was looking for his little one,
and that he was also attacked by a Soldier.
"Really?" replied the Soldier.
"He seemed to be angry with everything," added the Book.
"Sometimes it's easier to be angry," said the Soldier.

"How can you tell when you've grown up?"
asked the Soldier.

"You learn a little more every day,"
said the Book. "Today I learned
the difference between a soccer ball
and a basketball."

The Cat was having a nap.

The Bear came looking for the Rabbit.
It was time to find a home for the Egg.

When the Cat woke up, he cried, "Hooray!"
He had reached the end of his dream.
The Book clapped.
He was the kind of book
who liked happy endings.
Just then, the Stag appeared.

The Book asked him
whether he'd found his little one.
"No. Have you seen him, by any chance?
His ears are much bigger than mine,
he doesn't have antlers, and he
wants to grow up."
"The Rabbit?" asked the Soldier.
"He went that way."

Suddenly, the Stag spotted the Shadow.
By its side was the little Rabbit.
The Stag felt anxious.
He set off after them through the forest.

"Here I am, little Rabbit,
come back!" the Stag called out.
"Run, little Rabbit, faster, faster!"

The Rabbit heard him and ran
as fast as he could toward the Stag,
who suddenly turned and fled,
frightened by the Shadow.
But the Rabbit caught up with him.

"Don't worry, it's the Great Bear!
She's the one watching over us."

The anxious Stag looked at the Bear,
and the Bear smiled at him.
They recognized each other.
The Stag smiled back.

The Rabbit felt like a small house
was growing inside him.

Later, all together, they found the Egg's house.

As the afternoon drew to a close, there was a slight wind.
And three shadows perhaps.

This is the story of . . .

. . . a Soldier who isn't angry anymore,
a Book who learned something,
a Cat who reached the end of his dream,
and a Bear who watches silently over the night and her little ones.

"Did you manage to open the door
in your dream?" asked the Rabbit.
"Yes, and behind it were lots of kittens,
and you, and the Bear, and the Soldier, and
the Stag, and even the Book. A whole soccer team!"

This is the story of a Stag who doesn't feel anxious anymore
and a Rabbit who has grown up.

"I've grown up too, you know," said the Stag. "With you.
Thank you, little Rabbit, more than anything in the world."

31901062587938